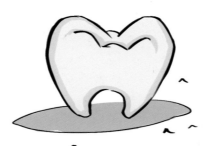

Tooth Ahoy!

Pirate Pete's Voyage to Healthy Teeth

Tooth Ahoy!

By Lisa Soesbe and Dr. Mitchell Kershner, ND

Lisa Soesbe and Dr. Mitchell Kershner, ND

Copyright © 2017 by Lisa Soesbe and Dr. Mitchell Kershner, ND

This book is a work of fiction. Names, characters, places, and incidents either are products of the author's imagination or are used fictitiously. Any resemblance to actual events or persons, living or dead, is entirely coincidental.

Illustrator: Jessica Pierce and Mandy Lansford

Executive Editor: Rachel Rehr

Design: 3SIXTY Marketing Studio - www.3sixtyprinting.com

Indigo River Publishing
3 West Garden Street Ste. 352
Pensacola, FL 32502
www.indigoriverpublishing.com

Ordering Information:

Quantity sales: Special discounts are available on quantity purchases by corporations, associations, and others. For details, contact the publisher at the address above.

Orders by U.S. trade bookstores and wholesalers: Please contact the publisher at the address above.

Printed in the United States of America

Library of Congress Control Number: 2017957110

ISBN: 978-1948080996

First Edition

With Indigo River Publishing, you can always expect great books, strong voices, and meaningful messages. Most importantly, you'll always find…words worth reading.

SEALY™

http://broward.floridahealth.gov

Pete the Pirate lived a normal pirate life, sailing the ocean blue with his trusty sidekick, Sweet P the Pineapple Parrot, and the rest of his pirate crew. Being a typical pirate, Pete and his crew ate a diet of the seven C's: candies, cookies, cake, cola, chips, chocolate, and cereal. Because of this diet of sweets and treats, Pete and his crew had horrible teeth.

One day as Pirate Pete and Sweet P were sailing along, one of Pete's teeth jumped out of his mouth!

Pete picked up the tooth, and, to his surprise, the tooth talked to him. "My name is Tony the Tooth, and I don't want to stay in your yucky mouth. You need to sail the ocean to find the true treasure and learn how to clean up your mouth and maintain a healthy diet. Only then will I get back in your mouth," said Tony. "Please make sure to keep me in a safe place," the tooth added. Pete put Tony in his pocket for safekeeping.

Pirate Pete wondered what it would take to clean up his mouth as Tony the Tooth had suggested. He gathered his crew to discuss going on a voyage to discover the secret treasure to a healthy mouth.

When Pirate Pete and the crew got together and went into town, they stopped at a shop to get their supplies. Pete told the shopkeeper about their voyage, so the shopkeeper gave Pete a special map.

When Pete and his crew returned to the ship,
they looked at the map and
figured out which islands
they would sail to.

Pete and his crew were excited about their journey and decided to have a party to celebrate their upcoming voyage. They feasted on the seven C's, again: cola, cereal, candy, cake, cookies, chips, and chocolate. The next morning, the crew woke up with the worst bellyaches.

Pete and his crew soon arrived at their first stop, Unfriendly Bacteria Island, where they were greeted by three scary bacteria. Pete introduced himself and his crew and asked the bacteria, "How do you help keep people's mouths healthy?"

The unfriendly bacteria said, "We don't keep mouths healthy! We like to eat sweets and treats! We cling to your teeth and turn into something called plaque, and then we dig holes in your teeth called cavities and make your gums weak. We hurt people's teeth!"

Saddened by what they had learned, Pete and his crew left Unfriendly Bacteria Island and set sail to their next destination.

"Squawk!" Sweet P screeched. "Head for the ship, Captain. Head for the ship!"

17

Pete and his crew arrived on Friendly Bacteria Island and were greeted by some friendly bacteria.
Pete asked, "What part do you play in people's mouths?"

The friendly bacteria said, "We help to protect your teeth and gums by preventing unfriendly bacteria from damaging your enamel. Plus we keep your breath smelling good! We also prevent unfriendly bacteria from digging holes, called cavities, in your teeth. All of this is possible only if we get the right kind of food and care."

18

Pete then asked, "What is the right kind of food and care?" The friendly bacteria told Pete and his crew how certain foods helped them to keep people's mouths healthy. Pete unrolled his treasure map, and the friendly bacteria pointed to another island, Fruit Island, where they would learn more.
Pete thanked the friendly bacteria,
and he and his crew set sail
for the next island.

20

Pete and his crew arrived at Fruit Island and were greeted by an apple, a pear, and a strawberry. Pete asked them, "How do you help keep people's mouths healthy?"

The apple told the crew, "We are nutritious and delicious! People even call us nature's candy. Fruits help you scrub, clean, and strengthen your teeth and gums. We also make you feel good and give you the right kind of energy to help you throughout the day."

Pete wondered how this "nature's candy" was different from the candy that he was used to eating.

"Nature's-squawk-candy?" Sweet P thought for a moment and flapped her wings excitedly. "Nature's candy! Squawk!"

The fruit told Pete and his crew to fill up baskets with fruit from the island so that they could have a taste of nature's candy on their journey.

Pirate Pete thanked them for the fruit, and he and the crew headed back to the ship to prepare for their next destination.

Pete and his crew arrived at Veggie Island and were greeted by a carrot, some broccoli, and a red pepper. Pete asked, "How do you help keep people's mouths healthy?"

Broccoli stood up and said, "We are vegetables, and we come in all kinds of shapes and colors. We are crunchy and tasty and can be used in many different ways. Chewing carrots, celery, and other hard vegetables helps make your teeth and gums even stronger."

"Vegetables keep your body healthy
and in good shape.

Eating vegetables also helps you build muscles.
Because vegetables have very little natural sugar in
them, they don't contribute to feeding the unfriendly
bacteria in your mouth."

Before Pete and his crew left Veggie Island, their new friends gave them several baskets of fresh-picked vegetables to eat on the way to their next destination. As Pete and his crew ate the vegetables, they were surprised at how good they tasted.

Try This At Home! With an adult's help
Set the Sail Salsa

Ingredients:

- 6 tomatoes, chopped
- 1-2 small jalapeno peppers
  (seeds optional)
- 1/2 onion
- 1/4-1/2 cup fresh cilantro
- 3 garlic cloves
- 1/2 to 2 teaspoons ground cumin
- 1 teaspoon sea salt
- 2 tablespoons lemon juice
  (about 1/2 lemon, juiced)

Instructions:

1. Add all vegetables into the bowl of a food processor. Pulse about 10 or so times and until all ingredients are combined and diced.
2. Taste the salsa and add more ingredients as desired.
3. Transfer to a bowl and enjoy with veggie chips of your choice. For best results refrigerate for 1 day before serving to allow flavors to mix well together. Salsa can keep for about a week in an airtight container or jar in the refrigerator.

Walk the Plank – Zucchini Chips
Makes about 20-30 chips

Ingredients:

- 1 large zucchini
- 2 tbsp. olive oil
- Kosher salt

Instructions:

1. Preheat oven to 225 degrees Fahrenheit. Line two large baking sheets with silicone baking mats or parchment paper.
2. Slice your zucchini on a mandolin or thinly slice with a knife.
3. After you slice your zucchini, place the slices on a sheet of paper towels and take another paper towel and sandwich the zucchini slices and press on them to remove excess liquid.
4. Line up the zucchini slices on the prepared baking sheet tightly next to each other in a straight line, making sure not to overlap them.
5. In a small bowl, pour your olive oil in and take a pastry brush to brush the olive oil on each zucchini slice.
6. Sprinkle a little salt throughout the baking sheet. Do not over season....a little salt goes a long way.
7. Bake for 2+ hours until they start to brown and aren't soggy and are crisp.
8. Let cool before removing and serve with Set the Sail Salsa.
9. If there are any leftover, keep in an airtight container for no more than 3 days.

Pirate Pete and his crew arrived at Toothbrush Island, where they were greeted by the Toothbrush Tribe. Pete asked, "How do you help to keep people's mouths healthy?"

"We are toothbrushes. Our bristles gently scrape food and something called plaque from your teeth, and we also help make your gums strong. By scrubbing your teeth, we keep unfriendly bacteria out of your mouth!"

Pete and his crew were amazed, as they had never seen such a tool before. The Toothbrush Tribe told them that it is very important to brush every tooth in your mouth, to brush the front of the teeth and the back of the teeth, and to brush gently, but thoroughly.

It is also very important to never share a toothbrush with anyone! After brushing, store your toothbrush upright so it can air dry.

The Toothbrush Tribe gave Pete and his crew some new toothbrushes to help them on their journey. Pete and his crew thanked them and set sail to Floss Island.

Arriving at Floss Island, Pete and Sweet P were greeted by a box of floss named Flossie and a floss pick named Fred. Pete asked, "How do you help keep people's mouths healthy?"

Flossie and Fred told Pete and his crew that they were two different kinds of dental floss and that both help remove food particles and plaque from between the teeth where a toothbrush cannot reach.

Sweet P whistled happily,
"They remove food and plaque! Squawk!"

"Our purpose is also to help gently
loosen and scrub unfriendly bacteria
from between your teeth. You should
floss once a day!" Fred said.

As Pete and the crew were leaving Floss Island, Flossie and Fred gave them some floss to practice with. "This is so much fun!" exclaimed Pete.

Flossie said, "If you think that's fun, you should visit Dental Island, where you'll find the real treasure." Pirate Pete and the crew got really excited for their next stop and waved goodbye to Flossie and Fred.

Maze

Help Pete and his crew reach their final destination, Dental Island, by following the maze.

Enter maze here...

 Dental Island

Pete and the crew arrived at Dental Island and were greeted by Dr. Smiley and her assistant, Tammy. Pete asked, "How do you help keep mouths healthy?"

Dr. Smiley said, "I am a dentist, and Tammy is a dental hygienist. A dental hygienist cleans your teeth and checks inside your mouth. A dentist can see things you cannot see. This is why it is important that you go to the dentist twice a year, so your dentist can make sure that you are practicing the right dental habits to prevent cavities and to help you if you are not.

"Going in for a checkup will lead you to your treasure. If you keep your mouth healthy, your teeth will last you a lifetime," explained Dr. Smiley.

"Wow, Dr. Smiley, now I really understand what it takes to have a healthy mouth," exclaimed Pete.

"Before we came here, our journey took us to Unfriendly Bacteria Island, Friendly Bacteria Island, Fruit Island, Veggie Island, Toothbrush Island, and Floss Island. We have learned so much after visiting these islands and have been working on taking better care of our mouths." Dr. Smiley was impressed and offered to take a look at the progress they had made.

Dr. Smiley looked into Pete's mouth and agreed that Pirate Pete had learned that by eating fruits and vegetables as well as brushing and flossing every day, he learned how to have a healthy mouth. "Except," Dr. Smiley said, "I see that you are missing a tooth."

Tony the Tooth jumped out of Pete's pocket at that moment. Tony told Pete how proud he was of him and that he was excited to get back into Pete's mouth.

Dr. Smiley said, "I can help with that!" and put Tony back where he belonged. Dr. Smiley and Tammy checked the rest of the crew, and they, too, had a good checkup because of what they had learned on their voyage.

"Well, I think you found your treasure, Pirate Pete and crew!" said Dr. Smiley.

"Squawk!" Sweet P flapped her wings excitedly. "Found your treasure, Captain! Found your treasure!"

Remember to eat less of the seven C's (cookies, candy, cereal, cola, chips, chocolate, and cake) and eat more fruits and veggies, brush your teeth twice a day, and floss once a day. By visiting the dentist twice a year for a checkup, you will find your own treasure — a healthy, happy mouth of teeth that will last you a lifetime.

Crossword

Crossword puzzle review - Now go on your own treasure hunt. You can find the answers to these questions throughout the book. (Answer key on page 44)

Across

4. Going in for a _____ with Dr. Smiley leads Pete and crew to their treasure.
5. Part of your mouth that teeth fit into.
6. Dental floss removes food _____ from the teeth.
8. Where did Pete and the crew meet Fred and Flossie?
9. What type of bacteria eats healthy fruits and veggies?
12. The tooth left Pirate Pete's mouth because he didn't want to live in a _____ mouth.

Down

1. What did Pete and his crew wake up with after celebrating their upcoming voyage?
2. On what island do Pete and the crew meet Dr. Smiley?
3. How should you store your toothbrush so it can air dry?
7. What type of bacteria eats sweets and treats?
10. Fruits make you feel good and give you the right kind of_____.
11. What was the name of the talking tooth?

Word Search

```
G S G P S C S T S A E P S D H
E M E H A A A E X I R L Q W I
J G W L L R L V V R V A V S N
M K A I B T R R I E Q Q C F U
I B V Y S A A O J T A U S M T
N A S I O G T L T C I E K R U
E U R O U V J E C A O E E L J
R B Q S P N A S G B B A S I S
A Y H C N U R C R E S V Q D T
L B R T E E T H I U V S N R I
S S K C A N S X R D H A Z E U
Q O T G P E M E N I L I J B R
I H L V J C R R P S R L U I F
P A M L B L U B I O N V N F W
B R O C C O L I M U S C L E J
```

ACID	CRUNCHY	MUSCLE	SNACKS
BACTERIA	FIBER	PARROT	SUGAR
BREATH	FRUITS	PLAQUE	TEETH
BRISTLES	ISLAND	SAIL	TREASURE
BROCCOLI	MAP	SALIVA	VEGETABLES
CAVITIES	MINERALS	SHIP	VOYAGE

42

Activity for Parents and Kids to do together

In this experiment, kids will learn how much hidden sugar is in popular drinks and how it can damage teeth!

Parents, please help the kids with this activity.

- Four clear disposable plastic cups or glass mason jars
- One can of cola
- One can of a popular energy drink
- One bottle of apple juice
- One bottle of a popular sports drink
- 3-5 Cups white sugar
- A teaspoon measuring spoon

1. Use a marker to label four cups with the following words: cola, energy drink, apple juice, and sports drink.

2. For each drink, look at the nutrition label on the bottle or can and calculate the amount of teaspoons of sugar that the grams of sugar in the drink amounts to. To do this divide the total grams of sugar in one serving by the number 4. The answer you get will tell you how many teaspoons of sugar are in that drink.

Nutrition Facts

1 servings per container

Serving size	1 bottle (491g)

Amount Per Serving

Calories	180

	% Daily Value*
Total Fat 0g	0%
Saturated Fat 0g	0%
Trans Fat 0g	
Sodium 20mg	1%
Total Carbohydrate 47g	17%
Dietary Fiber 0g	0%
Total Sugars 44g	
Includes 39g Added Sugars	78%
Protein 0g	0%

Not a significant source of cholesterol, vitamin D, calcium, iron, and potassium

*The % Daily Value (DV) tells you how much a nutrient in a serving of food contributes to a daily diet. 2,000 calories a day is used for general nutrition advice.

For example: According to this nutrition label here, this drink contains 44 grams of sugar. If you divide 44 by the number 4, you get 11 teaspoons of sugar.

3. As you figure out the number of teaspoons for each drink, scoop out how many teaspoons of sugar correspond with each drink and pour that amount in the appropriate cup. Set each cup next to the bottle or can of drink that corresponds with it and have a discussion with your child about this.

4. Was your child surprised at the amount of sugar in any of these drinks? Did they point out the amount of sugar in any of the drinks? Point out the number of servings in each of the containers and ask if they would stop drinking after one serving or if they would drink the whole container. Ask them based on what they learned from the book, if this amount of sugar would be good or bad for their teeth. Brainstorm with them some ideas of how, together, you can make healthier drink choices and encourage family members to do the same.

"By choosing our path, we choose our destination."

–Thomas S. Monson

Crossword Puzzle Answer Key:
Down: 1. bellyaches 2. Dental Island 3. upright 7. unfriendly 10. energy 11. Tony
Across: 4. checkup 5. gums 6. particles 8. Floss Island 9. friendly 12. yucky

About the Authors

Lisa Soesbe resides on the Treasure Coast of Florida. She is a wife and stay at home mother of two children, Leah and Jason. Frustration due to her children's frequent illnesses inspired her to make changes in their diet and lifestyle. After years of researching nutrition and holistic ways of treating her family, she realized that simple changes made a big difference, and these simple diet and lifestyle changes resulted in healthier children. Lisa started sharing her experience and results with her friends and family. Her books Tooth Ahoy!: Pirate Pete's Voyage to Healthy Teeth and One Small Bite for Kids are Lisa's way of sharing some of this information with the world.

Mitchell Kershner, a Naturopathic Doctor and Nutritionist, received his degree at National University of Naturopathic Medicine in Portland, Oregon. Upon graduating, Mitchell moved to Northern New Mexico where he was in private practice for 10 years. Dr. K, as his students referred to him, was an adjunct faculty professor at the University of New Mexico's nursing department. It was there he realized the importance of good nutrition as the foundation of health, especially in the children he was seeing in his private practice.

Our Mission is to make learning fun and tasty for the whole family.

To stay connected with us visit our website:

www.piratepetesvoyage.com

INDEX